THE AMAZING ADVENTURES OF THE

DC SUPER-PETS!™

Coast City Carnival Chaos

by Steve Korté

illustrated by Art Baltazar

PICTURE WINDOW BOOKS
a capstone imprint

Published by Picture Window Books, an imprint of Capstone.
1710 Roe Crest Drive
North Mankato, Minnesota 56003
www.capstonepub.com

Library of Congress Cataloging-in-Publication Data
Names: Korté, Steve, author. | Baltazar, Art, illustrator.
Title: Coast City carnival chaos / Steve Korté ; illustrated by Art Baltazar.
Description: North Mankato, Minnesota : Picture Window Books, an imprint
of Capstone, [2021] | Series: The amazing adventures of the DC super-pets |
Audience: Ages 5–7. | Audience: Grades K–1. | Summary: "It's B'dg's day off,
but heroes (and villains) never take a break. When a Red Lantern cat attacks
the super-squirrel's favorite carnival, the pint-sized super hero and his power
ring show up to save the day"—Provided by publisher.
Identifiers: LCCN 2020037774 (print) | LCCN 2020037775 (ebook) |
ISBN 9781515882534 (library binding) | ISBN 9781515883623 (paperback) |
ISBN 9781515891871 (pdf)
Subjects: CYAC: Cats—Fiction. | Squirrels—Fiction. | Superheroes—Fiction.
Classification: LCC PZ7.K8385 Met 2021 (print) | LCC PZ7.K8385 (ebook) |
DDC [E]—dc23
LC record available at https://lccn.loc.gov/2020037774
LC ebook record available at https://lccn.loc.gov/2020037775

Designed by Ted Williams
Design Elements by Shutterstock/SilverCircle

Printed and bound in the USA. 3837

TABLE OF CONTENTS

He is a pocket-sized hero
from outer space.

He wears an amazing power ring.

He is a member of the
Green Lantern Corps.

These are . . .

THE AMAZING
ADVENTURES OF
B'Dg the
Green Lantern!

CHAPTER 1

Amusement Park Alert!

A tiny, brown squirrel-like creature flies toward Earth.

It's B'dg, the hero from another planet! He is a member of the Green Lantern Corps. He fights crime.

A green power ring gives B'dg amazing powers. With the ring, he can create anything he can imagine.

B'dg zooms high above Coast City. He heads toward the amusement park. It's one of his favorite places to relax after a busy day of catching bad guys.

Suddenly, B'dg sees a blazing red light. It is coming from Dex-Starr, the Red Lantern cat. Red Lanterns get their power from anger. The evil cat is fighting with Green Lantern John Stewart.

Dex-Starr's power ring creates a thick red rope. It loops around John. He can't use his power ring to break the rope!

B'dg rushes to the rescue! He uses his own power ring. A large, green pair of scissors appears. He uses them to cut the rope and free John.

CHAPTER 2

Carnival Caper

Not far away, people are enjoying a Ferris wheel ride.

Dex-Starr blasts the Ferris wheel with his power ring. The ride freezes. People are trapped at the top!

John zooms into action to rescue the

riders. B'dg flies toward Dex-Starr.

Before B'dg can reach him, Dex-Starr

zaps a merry-go-round!

The wooden animals on the ride come to life. A horse, a pig, a giraffe, a rabbit, and a giant panda start jumping up and down.

The merry-go-round riders call out for help. John swoops in. The passengers are saved. But what will Dex-Starr do next?

B'dg has a plan. He sees a haunted house nearby.

"I'll bet you're too scared to follow me!" he calls to Dex-Starr.

B'dg rushes into the scary-looking old house. Dex-Starr is right behind him!

HAUNTED
HOUSE

CHAPTER 3

The Haunted House Hero

A tall skeleton stands inside the
haunted house. B'dg uses his power ring
to bring the skeleton to life.

The startled cat falls backward.

He tumbles down a staircase.

Dex-Starr topples into a dark room.

The room is full of cobwebs. It takes a

few moments for his eyes to adjust.

Suddenly, he sees something green

and glowing. It flies toward him. It's

a ghost!

The frightened cat lets out a yowl and tries to run.

Dex-Starr runs straight into a suit of armor! The armor falls over and breaks into pieces.

The armor's metal helmet lands on top of Dex-Starr. Only the evil cat's tail can be seen. It is angrily swishing from side to side.

Suddenly, the lights turn on. John
Stewart is there. His power ring blasts a
green ray around the helmet. Dex-Starr
is trapped!

John turns to the glowing ghost.

"That ghost costume was a great idea,"

he says. "You probably scared Dex-Starr

out of at least one of his nine lives!"

B'dg removes the sheet and grins at

John. Dex-Starr is one fraidy-cat who

won't be causing trouble any time soon.

AUTHOR!

Steve Korté is the author of many books for children and young adults. He worked at DC Comics for many years, editing more than 600 books about Superman, Batman, Wonder Woman, and the other heroes and villains in the DC Universe. He lives in New York City with his husband, Bill, and their super-cat, Duke.

ILLUSTRATOR!

Famous cartoonist Art Baltazar is the creative force behind *The New York Times* bestselling, Eisner Award-winning DC Comics' Tiny Titans; co-writer for Billy Batson and the Magic of Shazam, Young Justice, Green Lantern Animated (Comic); and artist/co-writer for the awesome Tiny Titans/Little Archie crossover, Superman Family Adventures, Super Powers, and Itty Bitty Hellboy! Art is one of the founders of Aw Yeah Comics comic shop and the ongoing comic series. Aw yeah, living the dream! He stays home and draws comics and never has to leave the house! He lives with his lovely wife, Rose, sons Sonny and Gordon, and daughter, Audrey! AW YEAH MAN! Visit him at www.artbaltazar.com

"Word Power"

amusement park (uh-MYOOZ-muhnt PARK)—an area that has rides, activities, and other fun things for people

armor (AR-muhr)—metal clothing that keeps the body safe from attacks

corps (KOR)—a group of people acting together or doing the same thing

Ferris wheel (FER-iss WEEL)—an amusement park ride with a huge wheel that turns; passenger cars hang on the wheel

haunted house (HAWN-tid HOWSS)—a house that is set up to be scary that people visit for fun

lantern (LAN-tuhrn)—a type of light or lamp

rescue (REH-skyoo)—to get someone or something out of danger

WRITING PROMPTS

1. Make a sign advertising the amusement park. Be sure to draw or add descriptions of the rides in the story.

2. Are you afraid of ghosts? Write a ghost story! Put B'dg in it to add to the adventure.

3. What do you think it was like for the people on the amusement park rides? Write a short story from one of their points of view.

DISCUSSION QUESTIONS

1. What is your favorite amusement park ride or attraction? Why? Compare your choice with a friend. Do you like the same ride?

2. If you had a power ring, how would you use it? What would you create?

3. Why do you think B'dg likes the amusement park so much?

THE AMAZING ADVENTURES OF THE DC SUPER-PETS!

Collect them all!